Michelle Obama
First Mom

by
Carole Boston Weatherford

illustrated by
Robert T. Barrett

Marshall Cavendish Children

Marshall Cavendish Corporation, 99 White Plains Road, Tarrytown, NY 10591

www.marshallcavendish.us/kids

Library of Congress Cataloging-in-Publication Data

Weatherford, Carole Boston, 1956–

Michelle Obama : first mom / by Carole Boston Weatherford ; illustrated by Robert Barrett. —, 1st ed.

p. cm.

Includes bibliographical references and index.

ISBN 978-0-7614-5640-7 (alk. paper)

1. Obama, Michelle, 1964– —Juvenile literature. 2. Presidents' spouses—United States—Biography—Juvenile literature.

3. Legislators' spouses—United States—Biography—Juvenile literature.

4. African American women lawyers—Illinois—Chicago—Biography—Juvenile literature.

5. Chicago (Ill.)—Biography—Juvenile literature I. Barrett, Robert, 1949– ill. II. Title.

E909.024W43 2010

973.932092—dc22

[B]

2009005953

The illustrations are rendered in oil on canvas.

Book design by Anahid Hamparian

Editor: Margery Cuyler

Printed in Malaysia (T)

First edition

1 3 5 6 4 2

To the first lady in my life, my mother—Carolyn W. Boston

—C.B.W.

To my granddaughters Mindee, Emma, Eliot, and Olivia—
may you each achieve greatness in your own way

—R.T.B.

Growing up on Chicago's South Side, Michelle did not know that her ancestors were slaves, or that her grandfather, a carpenter, was barred from joining a union because he was black, or that whites were fleeing South Shore because they didn't want black neighbors.

What Michelle *did* know was that her mother
stayed home with her and her big brother, Craig,
while her father worked the swing shift as a pump operator
for the city, and that the family had dinner together
every evening, and that she and Craig could watch
one hour of television on school nights.

Michelle did not mind the cramped apartment that her close-knit family shared. Her parents had divided the living room into three spaces—separate bedrooms for sister and brother and a study nook. That was ample space for them to know how important they were to their parents.

What Michelle sensed early on was the value

of education. Her parents taught her to read

by age four. Like Craig, she skipped second grade.

She took piano lessons from her great aunt,

who lived downstairs. But Michelle practiced so long

that her mother had to tell her when to stop.

The Robinson household was not all work, though. Michelle played with Barbie dolls and an Easy-Bake oven. With Craig, she played office and chess. Saturday nights, the family played board games like Chinese checkers. But Michelle hated losing. Sometimes, Craig let her win at Monopoly just so she'd keep playing with him.

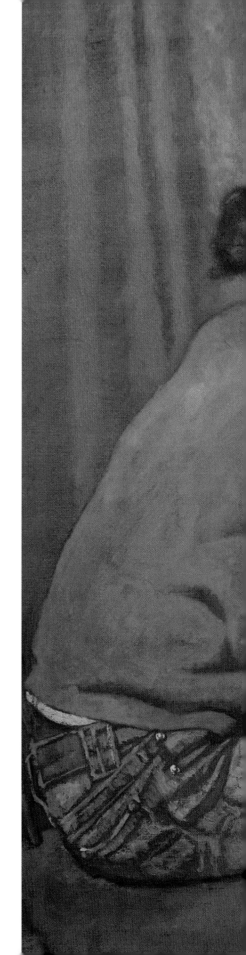

What her father refused to give in to was poor health.

At age thirty, he found out he had multiple sclerosis.

Michelle was a baby then—too young to know the toll

the disease would take. A former swimmer and boxer,

Fraser Robinson kept working, even after he needed

two canes to cross the street. He never complained. Never.

Just as he pushed himself past suffering, Fraser and his wife,

Marian, pushed their children to work hard, reach high.

In sixth grade, Michelle was picked for her school's gifted class.

That meant studying French and dissecting rodents

in a special biology class held at a college. In middle school,

she graduated second in her class—salutatorian.

What Michelle could not ignore were the changes around her.

Beyond the safe haven of her family's tiny apartment,

poverty and crime plagued the working-class neighborhood.

To keep from getting bullied on the way home from school,

Michelle used a different kind of smarts, appearing

to be tough, even though she was scared on the inside.

At age thirteen, Michelle had the guts and the grades

to attend a school miles away from home.

She rode a bus and an el train even on wintry days.

Whitney M. Young Magnet High School attracted the city's

best and brightest students. And Michelle shone:

honor roll, National Honor Society, student council treasurer.

What she wanted more than anything was to follow

her brother, Craig, to Princeton University.

Michelle was not deterred when a school counselor

said her test scores were too low for an Ivy League school.

She knew that she had what it took. She figured

if Craig could get in, so could she. And she was right.

After Princeton, she went on to Harvard Law School and was hired by one of Chicago's top law firms. She broke her own rule about dating coworkers when a summer associate she was mentoring would not take *no* for an answer. A year after losing her father, her hero, Michelle wed Barack Obama.

What she *knew* from the start was that she and Barack

shared not just love but also a desire to uplift others.

That desire led her from law to public service, to become

an executive at city hall, a university, and a hospital,

even though she and Barack both owed college loans.

That same spirit led him to run for the state senate.

The Obamas built not only successful careers

but also a family—two daughters, Malia and Sasha.

After Barack was elected to the U.S. Senate, Michelle

stayed in Chicago with their daughters to keep them grounded.

And when Barack ran for president, Michelle rushed home

from campaign appearances to kiss the girls good night.

What Michelle vows is that she is a mother first and a First Lady second. She may be Barack's rock, but she is her daughters' whole world, at least for now. Why we look up to her is not because she is stunning and stylish at nearly six feet tall, but because she is a walking, talking American success story.

And that we salute.